Egypt–

the ancient and mysterious land of priceless treasures—is the latest destination in your adventurous journeys with Indiana Jones™.

Your mission is to retrieve two ancient mummies stolen from the National Museum. This quest is doubly dangerous, for your opponents are the members of a strange cult that has existed for over a thousand years.

You'll face great danger everywhere you turn—from killer crocodiles to fatal felines and more. You will choose your actions and decide your fate by following directions at the bottom of each page.

Are you up to the task? You'd better be, because only the right choices will get you home safely.

The wrong choices are too scary to contemplate!

Best of luck. And watch your step...

INDIANA JONES

JONES ™

and the

CULT OF THE
MUMMY'S CRYPT

by R. L. STINE

Illustrated by DAVID B. MATTINGLY

BALLANTINE BOOKS ● NEW YORK

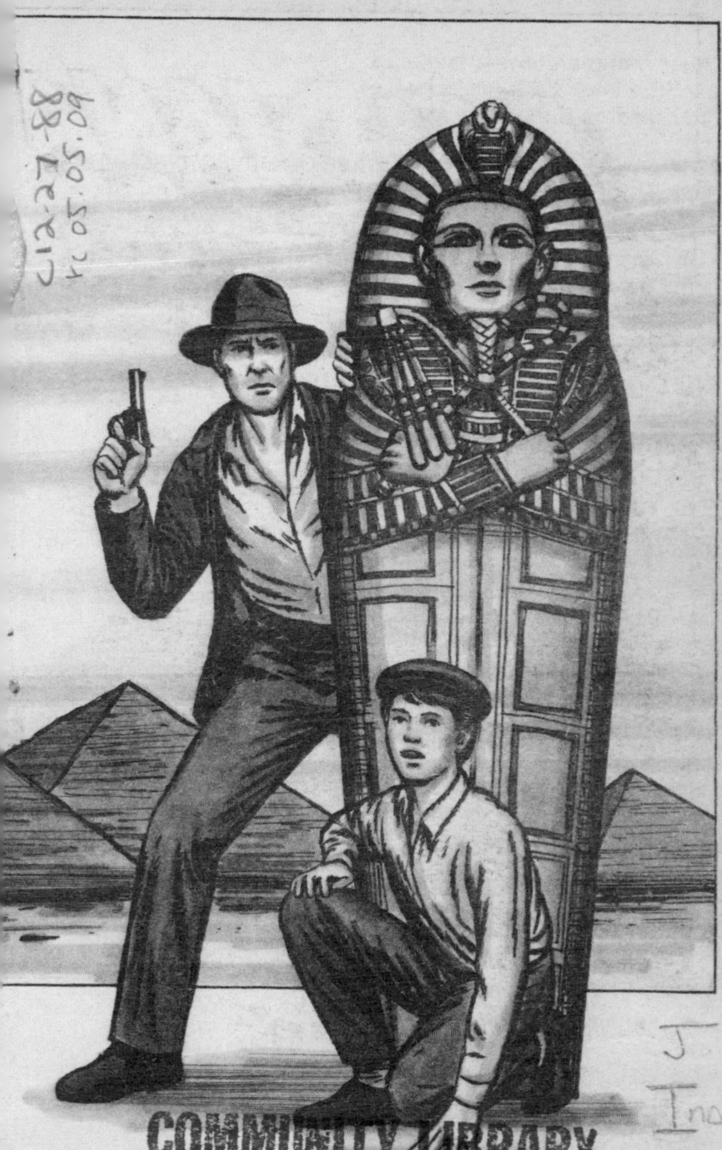

Other Indiana Jones™ books in
the Find Your Fate™. Series
Published by Ballantine Books:

INDIANA JONES™ AND THE CURSE OF HORROR ISLAND
INDIANA JONES™ AND THE LOST TREASURE OF SHEBA
INDIANA JONES™ AND THE GIANTS OF THE SILVER
TOWER
INDIANA JONES™ AND THE EYES OF THE FATES
INDIANA JONES™ AND THE CUP OF THE VAMPIRE
INDIANA JONES™ AND THE LEGION OF DEATH
INDIANA JONES™ AND THE CULT OF THE MUMMY'S
CRYPT
INDIANA JONES™ AND THE DRAGON OF VENGEANCE
INDIANA JONES™ AND THE GOLD OF GENGHIS KAHN

RLI: $\frac{\text{VL: 5 + up}}{\text{IL: 5 + up}}$

Library of Congress Catalog Card Number: 84-91747

ISBN 0-345-33869-3

Designed by Gene Siegel

Cover and interior art by David B. Mattingly

Manufactured in the United States of America

First Edition: February 1985
Third Printing: February 1986

INDIANA JONES™

and the

CULT OF THE MUMMY'S CRYPT

Find Your Fate™• #7

**Cairo, Egypt
June 1934**

"Watch out, kid!" Indiana Jones yells.

You leap out of the way as a camel caravan comes pounding through the narrow street. The camels, laden with bulging straw baskets of dates and figs, gallop past, kicking up a thick cloud of dust that floats toward the crowded, outdoor market across from you. You turn your head away from the dust. Behind you, you see a purple-domed mosque surrounded by a low brick wall. Bearded men in long, colorful caftans push past you, ignoring the dust.

"We're a long way from home, kid," Indy says, lifting his battered hat to scratch his head. "If your parents knew I dragged you here, they'd murder me!"

"Well...they wanted me to have an exciting summer vacation," you tell your cousin. "That's why they sent me to stay with you."

Indy grins and begins to walk quickly up the crowded street. A veiled woman dressed in black passes by quickly. She turns her eyes away from yours. "This is going to be very educational," you tell Indy, struggling to keep up with him and not lose him in the crowd.

You don't realize just *how* educational it's going to be!

....

Turn to page 2.

1

Ka-whommmmp!

A concrete boulder hits the street and shatters just a few inches in front of you.

Squinting against the bright sun, you and Indy both look up. There is someone standing on the flat roof of a five-story building, the tallest on the street. He's holding another boulder above his head, and he's about to toss it down onto you!

Ka-whommmp!

This one lands even closer. The narrow street echoes with the screams of men and women as they run to get out of the way. A cart overturns, spilling its load of oranges, which tumble and roll past your feet.

"What's going on?" you shout.

"Someone's trying to deliver a message to us," Indy says. "And I don't think it's 'Welcome to Egypt'!"

What's your next move? Try to get up to the roof and confront this guy? Or duck into the nearest building to get out of the line of fire?

··
Climb up to the roof? Turn to page 33.
Duck into the building? Turn to page 42.

2

The chamber walls are covered with bright orange-and-red tapestries, depicting the splendor of ancient Egypt. A long orange carpet runs down the center of the vast room. It leads to a straight-backed golden throne. On the throne sits a fierce-looking man with long black hair. He is wrapped in a sparkling white robe. He carries a golden scepter. On his head he wears a crown of gold with green and red jewels.

"Bow down before the New Pharaoh!" a voice yells behind you. Rough hands shove you down to the floor.

You raise your head and look around. The room is filled with servants of the New Pharaoh, all dressed in black robes.

"Sorry to crash your costume party," Indy yells to the man on the throne. "But I believe you may have mistakenly taken a few things that belong to us—a few mummies, to be exact!"

"Do not dare to speak to the New Pharaoh!" the voice behind you cries, and hands shove Indy's face into the floor.

"Shall I kill them now, Emperor?"

Turn to page 35.

On contact with Indy, the ancient sword crumbles into dust. Indy and the fake mummy both stare at each other in disbelief.

Then Indy reaches forward and rips the gauze off the mummy's face.

"Dr. Salaam!" you cry.

"Now, you will surely die, Jones!" Salaam cries. "My little explosion and fake blood didn't throw you off the track! Too bad for you!"

"Salaam, you don't mean to tell me you really believe this mumbo jumbo about bringing mummies back to life," Indy says. "What are you really up to out here?"

Before Salaam can answer, you hear a deafening roar behind you. Startled, you turn around to see a six-foot-high wall of water rushing through the chamber entrance. The water is up to your ankles before you realize what is happening!

Turn to page 15.

Indy feels around on the cold, wet wall until he finds a lever. He pulls it and a door slowly creaks open. The three of you burst through it at once. You find yourselves in a vast, dimly lit room of marble floors and walls, filled with glass display cases and ancient stone mummy cases.

"We're in the mummy room," Marla Evans says in surprise. "And look—a mummy has been stolen from that sarcophagus!"

"There's a trail of blood on the floor," you say. "They must have carried Salaam through here."

"The bombing and locking us in the office were all part of their plot to steal a mummy," Indy says, searching the room for other clues. "What I don't understand is why are they dragging Salaam along with them?"

"Another mummy is missing," Marla says. "I can't believe it—two of them! They're worth millions!"

"They'll be worth more when they're alive!" you comment.

Indy frowns at you. "Not funny, kid."

The three of you follow the trail of blood past row after row of dark mummy cases into the next room, the ancient weapons room. The walls are lined with metal spears.

Two men in long black robes and black turbans are standing across the room. When they see you enter, they each pick up one of the ancient spears from a display case and charge toward you, screaming angrily as they attack!

Turn to page 38.

5

You and Indy pull yourselves out of the pit.

The tigers have chosen another victim. A man screams and falls beneath their claws. Shots ring out. They miss the tigers and ricochet off the ancient walls.

The New Pharaoh still stands frozen in terror. Indy rushes up behind him and grabs him. You pick up a gun from a fallen servant.

"Okay, let's get going!" Indy yells.

Indy stands behind the New Pharaoh, using him as a shield. You get right behind Indy. Quickly you make your way through the throng of terrified servants.

You walk out of the chamber, shoving the New Pharaoh in front of you. He seems to have crumbled completely in the face of his cowardice.

You make your way through the torch-lit tunnels of the pyramid toward the entrance...

...and run into Marla Evans and several Cairo policemen.

"We found Dr. Salaam. They were keeping him prisoner in another chamber," she says. "Are you okay?"

"Peachy," Indy tells her. "Tell your cop friends they've got a couple of tigers to arrest in there." He turns to you. "Guess this adventure is just about over, kid."

You frown and look up at him. "Gee, Indy, what do we do next?"

THE END

"Stop right there!" Indy yells at the top of his lungs, startling the men in black robes.

Indy doesn't give them time to react. He springs from the top of the carton and leaps onto one of the cult members, knocking the pistol from his hand.

The man grabs at Indy and misses.

Indy dives to the floor and tries to grab the pistol. The gun slides across the floor, out of reach.

Two men leap onto Indy and begin punching him. All three are rolling around on the floor in a desperate wrestling match.

Can Indy possibly win this match??

Turn to page 26.

Suddenly Indy breaks free from the black-robed man who holds him. He leaps over the altar and grabs the handle of the black pot.

"AAAAAAIIIIIIEEEEEE!"

Indy falls to the floor, holding his hand and writhing in agony.

"Evidently you're not a very experienced cook," the fake mummy says, laughing. "You should use a potholder when you pick up a hot pot!"

Since everyone is staring at Indy, who is still down on the floor holding his burning hand, you decide to make a run for it. Your heart pounding, you turn and break toward the door.

"Get him—but don't damage his brain!" the mummy cries.

You're almost to the door when something hits you in the back. The pain is overwhelming. You fall to the floor.

The last things you see are the lilies beside the altar. Then everything goes black.

When you awaken, you and Indy are tied down to the altar. The fake mummy stands over you. Beside him stands a man whose face is covered by a white surgical mask. In his right hand he holds a scalpel!

Turn to page 34.

You reach the pyramid entrance and run inside. It is hot, musty, and dark. Now you turn and look to the truck to see if you're being followed.

You're not. The man you heard yelling was upset because one of the mummies was dropped from the truck. You watch the black-robed men struggle to remove the second mummy.

"We can't stand here sightseeing, kid," Indy says. "We've got to find a good hiding place in here until we can figure out what to do with these clowns."

Your eyes are slowly adjusting to the darkness. There are torches lining the walls of the entrance chamber. And on the far wall you can make out three doorways.

"Which way do we go?" you ask Indy, still trying to catch your breath from your dash into the pyramid.

"Pick a doorway," Indy said. "Maybe we'll get lucky."

Which do you choose?

The one on the left? Turn to page 28.
The one in the middle? Turn to page 39.
The one on the right? Turn to page 53.

Indy waits until the men are only a few feet away. Then he leaps onto the nearest one, grabs his scarf, and spins him around with it. The man stumbles into his nearest companion, and the two men go sprawling to the ground.

You pick up Indy's pistol from the spot where you dropped it, but the third man kicks it away from you.

Indy plows into him, grabs his arm, and struggles to get his pistol. They wrestle to the ground, then roll over and over until they reach the edge of the roof.

"Indy! Look out!" you cry, seeing that they are both about to topple over the side.

Indy and the robed man suddenly freeze. They seem to be looking behind you.

You turn and see four men in uniform climbing onto the roof. One of them yells out something in Arabic. These four men are carrying pistols too.

"Cairo police guards!" Indy yells, climbing to his feet.

Do you take this opportunity to escape and let the police fight it out with the three robed men? Or do you think it would be wiser to stop and explain to the police that these men attacked you?

....

Escape? Turn to page 31.
Explain? Turn to page 41.

11

A mummy staggers forward and drops onto your back!

You feel as if you're being smothered by the four-thousand-year-old stench. You roll out from under the decaying creature. You see Indy still struggling in the grasp of another mummy, growing weaker as the mummy tightens its powerful grip.

You throw yourself forward, reaching for the papyrus, reaching, reaching...

...and you grab it!

You dodge away from a black-robed man who tries to tear it from your hands.

"I've got it! I've got it!" you scream, holding the papyrus high above your head.

But what does having the papyrus in your possession mean? Will it really help you?

Turn to page 29.

Your three captors lead you through the dark, twisting passages of the pyramid into a large, well-lit chamber. In the center of the chamber stands an altar, surrounded by pots of fresh white lilies. To the left of the altar stand six ancient mummies, all in their cases.

"There are the two mummies from the National Museum," Indy mutters to you. His voice echoes off the walls of the chamber, even though he speaks quietly. "I recognize some of the others. They are all stolen."

Behind the altar stands a large black pot suspended over hot coals. A thick liquid simmers in the pot.

Next to the pot stands another mummy.

As your captors force you to walk closer to the altar, the mummy turns and begins to walk toward you.

Turn to page 79.

These mummies do not move. They are propped against wooden crates. "What are they doing here?" Marla asks, her eyes wild with fear. She has lost all of her calm and composure.

Indy takes a close look. "These mummies are all stolen," he says. "Here are the two from the National Museum."

"Mission accomplished!" you say, trying to sound cheerful.

"Not quite," Indy says grimly. "Now we've got to get them out of here. The Cult of Rhamahr is obviously headquartered right here in the Cairo Museum in these secret chambers. And now I remember about the cats!"

"What do you mean?" you ask him.

"More than a thousand years ago cult members believed they could transfer the souls from certain cats into the bodies of mummies to bring the mummies back to life. The cats we found back in that chamber were probably used to—"

Indy doesn't finish his sentence.

Your hear footsteps approaching.

Someone is entering the chamber!

Turn to page 32.

"It's the Nile! It's flooding its banks!" Indy yells over the roar of the water.

Dr. Salaam and his guards flee in panic. They try to run through the wave to the chamber doorway, but they are driven back by the powerful force of the onrushing water.

"I can't swim!" Salaam yells, the water already up to his waist.

"The mummies!" Indy cries, seeing the precious artifacts being covered with water. He begins to wade through the rising water toward them. Then he stops. "Maybe we'd be smarter to save ourselves."

You must decide. Try to save the mummies first—or save yourselves before the water is over your heads?

Save the mummies? Turn to page 46.
Save yourselves? Turn to page 77.

You run forward and, with all your strength, push over one of the barrels filled with wheat. The barrel falls onto Abdul's legs. He stumbles forward. The cobra slides out of his hand and onto the floor.

Indy jumps away from the two-headed snake. Abdul leaps onto Indy, punching him in the stomach with both hands. They pull each other to the ground, wrestling in the spilled wheat.

The cobra arches its two heads and prepares to attack....

Both heads bite into their victim at once.

"AAAAIIIIIII!" The vast warehouse echoes with his screams.

Turn to page 106.

"BATS!" Indy cries.

You can barely make out the flapping wings of dozens of bats in the darkness of the narrow passage.

"If I weren't so terrified, I'd scream," Marla says, her voice a shaky whisper.

And then she screams.

A bat has grabbed on to her shoulders. Its wide wings beat furiously about her head.

Indy removes the bullwhip from his shoulder, holds it up in the air, and cracks it.

The bat drops its hold on Marla. Indy cracks the whip again. The bats, highly sensitive to sound, flap a hasty retreat. The fluttering fades in the distance.

"They'll be back," Indy says.

Marla has covered her face with her hands. "I'm so embarrassed that I screamed," she says.

"We don't have time to be embarrassed. If we're going to catch up with whoever kidnapped Salaam and locked us in the office, we gotta get moving," Indy says.

"Maybe the gas is gone. Maybe we can go back through the office," you say, thinking of the bats that await ahead in the darkness.

You must decide which way to go.

Keep going forward? Turn to page 27.

Get out of the dark tunnel and go back to the office? Turn to page 54.

17

You stand side by side and lower your torches to the floor. At first the scorpions don't seem to notice.

You take a step forward.

A scorpion crunches under your foot.

The scorpions beneath the flame of your torch scurry backward. You take another step, keeping the torch flame in front of you on the floor.

The scorpions are clearing a path. The torches are keeping them back.

Just a few more steps... and you will be back at the entranceway.

SNAP!

A scorpion snaps its tail toward you, attempting a venomous sting from behind. It misses by less than half an inch.

You've made it! You're back in the entrance chamber. The black-robed men carrying the stolen mummies are about to enter the pyramid.

You still have two doorways left to explore. Will you choose the one in the middle? Or the one on the right? Quick—make your choice before you are spotted!

The middle doorway? Turn to page 39.
The doorway on the right? Turn to page 53.

Marla seems totally surprised to see anyone in the room. Her eyes grow even wider when she realizes that the ancient mummies are advancing toward you. She utters a scream...

...which is cut short by a hand around her mouth. And one of the black-robed men grabs her and pulls her away from the secret doorway.

"The papyrus! Grab it!" she manages to cry out before the man puts his hand over her mouth again.

The doorway she has just come through is only a few yards away from you. Should you make an attempt to run to it? Or should you pick up the papyrus?

You must decide.

Run for the secret doorway? Turn to page 50.

Try to pick up the papyrus? Turn to page 58.

Indy reaches the truck first. He grabs a
handle on the back door and pulls himself up
onto the rear bumper. Then he reaches a hand
out toward you. You grab it and jump as hard
as you can. Your feet hit the bumper. You both
grab on to a rack on top of the truck and hold
on for dear life.

Marla is running hard toward the truck.
Indy stretches a hand to her. She reaches for
it...

...and falls.

The truck picks up speed. She is left behind.

"That was a good try," Indy says with ad-
miration. "She's got spirit. She just doesn't know
it! I hope she'll be okay."

In a few minutes the city disappears behind you. Soon you are surrounded by yellow sand. "Look over there," Indy says, pointing. "See that strip of dark blue on the horizon?"

You see it, a shimmering line of blue against the yellow sand.

"That's the Nile. Right out of the history books," Indy says. "And you might be lucky enough to see the river flood. It's a few weeks overdue. Supposed to be quite a sight."

How can Indy talk so calmly? The truck bumps across the desert. You hold on tightly, ignoring the pain in your arms, worrying what will happen when the truck stops.

Turn to page 55.

You duck down behind the carton and hope that you are not detected. You hear the black-robed men scurrying about the room, speaking in low voices.

You peek around the carton and see that they have gathered up all of the mummies. They pull them out of the chamber.

The Cairo policemen are still lying on the floor, bound and gagged, unable to move.

The four men in black robes, having removed all the mummies, turn to leave. You hear one of them say something in Arabic. The others laugh. Then a door slams behind them.

"What was that?" you ask Indy. "What did he say that was so funny?"

"I don't exactly get the joke," Indy says grimly. "He said that now that the mummies were removed, they were going to seal up this room forever."

You don't get the joke either. It doesn't strike you at all funny. Listening to the men working on the other side of the door to close it up forever, you realize that your fate is sealed and this adventure has reached its

END.

Indy raises his bullwhip. But an ancient gauzed hand springs forward and knocks it from his grasp.

The odor is overpowering now. Marla covers her nose and backs toward the door. The cats are screeching and crying.

Why are the cats in this secret chamber? Do they have something to do with the power that brought the mummies back to life? You will not find out.

The mummies surround you and grasp you in their powerful arms.

This adventure has a gripping ending. Unfortunately *you* are the ones being gripped!

Evidently they intend to squeeze all the drama they can out of this story.

Better close the book. This is definitely

THE END.

A tall man wearing a black robe steps out of the shadows. He is carrying something in his hands. "Jones, thank you for stepping into this trap," he says quietly. "I am afraid you will not be allowed to complete your mission here in Egypt."

"Abdul!" Indy cries, recognizing the man immediately. "What an unpleasant surprise. I'd heard you were mixed up in some sort of black-magic cult. You ought to be embarrassed—a scientist of your stature! Tsk, tsk."

"I wish I could allow you to live so that you might learn to respect this cult, Jones. But it is out of the question." Abdul steps closer. You and Indy gasp as you see what he is carrying. It is a cobra. No—it is...

...a *two-headed* cobra!

Indy backs away. His hands are trembling. His eyes are filled with fear. Snakes are the things that terrify Indiana Jones the most. And this man named Abdul seems to know that.

"Unusual little snake, isn't it, Jones?" Abdul cries, jabbing the two-headed cobra at Indy. "It has an unusual bite, too. Ha, ha!"

You can see that Indy is paralyzed with fear. If you're going to get out of this dark warehouse alive, it's going to be up to YOU!

But what can you do?

Turn to page 16.

You hold the flame of the torch up to the door. The dry wood catches fire immediately. The door burns quickly. You kick it in and the burning wood shatters and falls to the ground.

Except for a few small smoldering pieces of wood, the fire disappears almost as quickly as it burned. "Okay—we can get outta here!" you call to Indy.

"Nice goin', kid," he says, finally turning away from the tigers, who pace back and forth against the far wall. "But we've got one little problem. If we leave, what's to keep the tigers from following?"

Indy has a good point. Maybe burning down the door wasn't such a good idea.

"Stop right there!" a voice cries from outside the chamber. "Shamir, I have found the two Americans!"

Through the doorway you see a black-robed man running toward you, pistol in hand.

Turn to page 56.

The two cult members who are not fighting stand and watch as Indy and their two cohorts wrestle around on the floor. Suddenly they seem to realize that Indy is not their only foe in the room.

One of them runs over and tries to grab Marla, who backs away in surprise. You reach your foot out, and the man trips over it, falling to the floor, his robes tangled around him. The other one is coming after YOU now!

"Indy, help!" you cry, realizing you are no match for this angry cult member.

But Indy is too involved in his own fight to hear you!

The man grabs you by the shoulders and lifts you off the ground. Marla screams!

Turn to page 37.

The three of you hurry through the dark passage. You keep listening for the bats to return, but they seem to have retreated to a different area of the museum.

"Did Dr. Salaam ever mention this passage to you?" Indy asks Marla.

"No, never," she replies.

"Who else would know this museum well enough to know about it?" Indy asked.

"I—I don't know," she answers, struggling to keep up.

"What about that cult you mentioned?" you ask.

"The Cult of Rhamahr believed they could bring mummies back to life. But that was a thousand years ago," says Indy as you make your way through the darkness.

"Could they do it?"

"I'd be real surprised," Indy said. "I'm even more surprised that people are falling for that nonsense all over again in 1934!"

"But it would explain why the mummies were stolen from your museum back home," Marla says.

"To be brought back to life?" Indy smiles.

His smile is cut short. All three of you discover at once that the narrow passage ends at a solid wall. There is no exit.

Turn to page 5.

You each grab a torch and make your way into a dark chamber on the left. You hear a curious scratching sound.

You walk close together in a straight line. "This chamber has got to lead somewhere," Indy says, although his voice is not exactly confident.

"What is that scratching sound?" you ask. You feel something crackly under your shoes.

You hold your torches down to the floor.

SCORPIONS!

Hundreds of them crawl along the floor. The cult members must have put them here to keep out intruders.

"Their sting can be deadly," you say, standing on tiptoes. "I read about them in a science book."

"Well, here they are in person," Indy said dryly. "You *said* this trip was going to be educational." He holds his torch up high. "There's a low beam up there," he says. "Maybe I can loop my whip around it, and we can swing ourselves out of here."

"Why don't we just use our torches to burn a path back?" you suggest.

"The scorpions will get out of our way—maybe." A scorpion at your feet attempts to sting. It stings your shoe. You jump away.

What will you try?

....

Swing out of the chamber on the whip? Turn to page 45.

Use the torches to burn your way out? Turn to page 18.

28

You hold the papyrus high above your head.

Everyone in the room freezes.

The mummies stop in their tracks and turn toward you.

Indy breaks free of the mummy that was strangling him. It makes no attempt to recapture him.

The black-robed men all come after you now. "Hold on to the papyrus!" Marla yells. "The holder of the papyrus is master over the mummies!"

You grasp the papyrus tightly in your hand and try to run from the black-robed men, who are desperate to retrieve it. You trip over a mummy case. You fall backward.

In a split second you must decide: Should you clutch the papyrus to you as you fall or try to toss it to Indy?

Keep it? Turn to page 52.
Toss it? Turn to page 82.

The policemen seem confused. They cannot figure out what you are all doing on this rooftop. Then one of them spots the crumpled body of the huge man.

"Uh-oh. We're in for it now," Indy says. "Don't wait, kid—and don't look. Just jump!"

You and Indy run to the edge of the roof...
...and leap off!

In the half-second as you begin to fall, you realize that you have not jumped far enough to reach the roof of the next building. You are about to plunge five stories to the street below!

Turn to page 57.

You duck down behind a large carton. You peer over the side and see four men in black robes enter the room. They have taken the two Cairo policemen as prisoners and have bound and gagged them. They shove the policemen roughly to the floor.

Indy reaches for his bullwhip, but he has left it on the floor of the cats' chamber. "We've gotta fight these guys to get our mummies back," Indy whispers.

"But we have no weapons," Marla protests. "We'd better just hide here until they go away."

You must decide what to do.

....

Hide? Turn to page 22.
Fight? Turn to page 7.

You run around to the side of the building. "Look, Indy—stairs!" you cry. "Maybe they lead up to the roof!"

"Let's go!" Indy yells.

As you race up the narrow stone steps the cries from the street below still echo off the low buildings.

Out of breath, you reach the top and step out onto the roof. Standing there waiting to greet you is the biggest man you've ever seen. He must be seven feet tall! He's wearing a black caftan that billows around him like a circus tent. His powerful muscles bulge as he holds a concrete boulder over his black-turbaned head.

He rears up to hurl it at you!

Turn to page 48.

"How are you doin', kid?" Indy asks. "The brick that guy threw at you was pretty hefty."

"I've felt better," you tell him. "How are you going to get us out of this one?"

Indy looks down at the wires wrapped round his arms, chest, and legs. "I'm not sure yet," he says.

"You'll think of something," you say, but your voice lacks confidence.

"Put them to sleep," the fake mummy commands the doctor. "Our ancestors have been prepared. They await their new brains."

The surgeon bends low and extends a gas mask to your face. You turn your head from side to side, struggling to avoid the oblivion that awaits you. But the doctor is strong. He clamps the mask over your face.

You hold your breath. You will force yourself not to breathe.

Then you hear a voice shouting, "Stop right there! Everybody freeze!"

Turn to page 70.

The New Pharaoh slowly rises from his throne. All the black-robed servants in the chamber bow their heads twice and then chant a short prayer in what must be an ancient Egyptian language.

You notice for the first time that there are mummies standing upright in open mummy cases on both sides of the New Pharaoh's golden throne.

The Chamber grows silent as the New Pharaoh begins to speak in a powerful voice that echoes off the ancient brick walls.

"The invaders of the Sacred Hall of Rhamahr must die!" the New Pharaoh yells, raising his scepter above his head. "I have not taken anything of yours, American thief! I have reclaimed my ancestors! All of our ancestors will return home, and all of our ancestors will return to life—to help me as I lead, to serve me as I reign! For I am the New Pharaoh of Egypt. And the New Pharaoh will lead the people of Egypt— the ancient people as well as the people of to-day—to our place of sovereignty over the world!"

A long ear-shattering cheer rises up from the servants. "He's nuts!" you yell to Indy.

"Kid, you're a master of understatement," Indy says. "The question is, do we try to make our escape now? Or do we wait until King Baloney comes a little closer to us?"

....

Try to escape now? Turn to page 72.
Wait until you can grab the New Pharaoh?
Turn to page 86.

All three of you stare at the spot where the wounded Salaam had been lying. All that remains is a pool of blood.

"Kidnapped!" Marla cries. She shudders. You can see that she is using all her self-control to keep from getting hysterical.

"How could he have been kidnapped? No one came into this room!" Indy says. "Unless there's a trap door in here." He begins to search the wall and floor.

"We'll never find it in time," says Marla shakily.

"Let's try the window instead," you suggest, choking from the gas. Your eyes are burning so badly you can barely see.

"We have less than a minute," Indy says flatly. You wonder how he can be so calm.

You must decide which way to try to escape.

Look for a trap door or a secret exit in the wall? Turn to page 47.

Try to escape through the window? Turn to page 59.

The man lifts you up in the air and is about to toss you head first across the room...

...but he stops.

You slide out of his hands and realize he isn't looking at you anymore.

He is looking toward the doorway...where eight ancient mummies are stumbling in at surprising speed!

Indy rolls away from the men he was battling and pulls you and Marla back. The four cult members stand frozen in fear. When they finally turn to run, it is too late. The mummies grab them up in their powerful arms.

The cult members are screaming in Arabic, but their words have no effect!

Indy rushes to untie the Cairo policemen. They stare in horror as the mummies crush their black-robed victims, then slump to the floor, lifeless and still.

A few minutes later you and Indy check the chamber containing the caged cats. The cats are all lying dead in their cages. "The cult's power is ended," Indy says darkly. "The mummies will not walk again."

Then Indy's mood suddenly brightens. "I guess we've done our job," he says. "We'll arrange to have the National Museum's mummies sent home. Then maybe we'll go out and buy you some souvenirs to take home."

"Uh...no, thanks, Indy," you say with a grin. "I really don't think I'll have any trouble remembering this trip!"

THE END

37

You grab one of the ancient spears from the wall and toss it to Indy. Marla backs into a corner, almost tumbling into the empty mummy sarcophagus as Indy charges.

You look away as you hear the clang of spear against ancient spear. When you look back, one of the black-robed men is on the floor writhing in pain.

Indy leaps over him and prepares to deal with the other attacker. The two men struggle, plunging their ancient weapons at each other, until...

...Indy's spear breaks in two!

Turn to page 66.

There are footsteps behind you. You have no time to hesitate. The two of you walk quickly through the middle doorway.

It leads into a long, winding tunnel. The tunnel is completely dark, but you and Indy have taken torches from the entrance chamber. The torches flicker and crackle in the thin, ancient air.

"This is creepy," you tell Indy.

"It's supposed to be creepy," Indy says. "The Pharaohs who built these pyramids didn't want people walking around in them. They wanted to be left alone for eternity."

What are those footsteps you hear behind you?

"Don't be afraid, kid," Indy says. "It was only a rat."

Only a rat?! Turn to page 71.

"WALK, MUMMIES! WALK, ANCESTORS! LIVE AGAIN! IN THE NEW EGYPT, IN *MY* NEW EGYPT!"

The New Pharaoh waves his scepter. His words echo off the ancient walls.

The mummies remain stiff and unmoving, frozen in the positions they have held for four thousand years.

Another wave of the scepter. The mummies do not move.

Silence.

The silence is broken by an angry cry from the throng of black-robed servants and guards: "The New Pharaoh is a fraud! We have been betrayed!"

Others take up the cry. Weapons are raised. The New Pharaoh is captured. A guard grabs his scepter. You turn away as the New Pharaoh is beaten again and again with his own scepter.

Someone releases you and Indy. "Let's get outta here!" Indy calls over the angry cries of revolt in the chamber.

A black-robed guard leads you out of the chamber, to the small room where Dr. Salaam has been held prisoner. Salaam looks weak, but he is conscious and very glad to see you.

A few minutes later you are on your way back to Cairo. The screams of the rioters still ring in your ears. "We'll pick up our mummies when the rioting has stopped," Indy says, definitely pleased with the results of the day. "I guess they won't come walking to find *us*!"

THE END

Indy calls out a few words of explanations to the four Cairo policemen, but they ignore him.

"Achmed, have these two Americans caused you difficulty?" the police lieutenant asks one of the robed men. He is speaking in English, obviously for your benefit.

"I wish to file a formal complaint against these foreigners," the robed man says. "They have murdered my companion here," he says sadly, pointing to the giant body.

"Now, wait a minute!" Indy cries angrily. "The kid and I are here to retrieve some stolen mummies. We just arrived in this country and we don't know anything about— OWWWWWWWWWWW!"

The police lieutenant hits Indy over the head with the butt of his pistol. Indy staggers back, then stares at the policemen in silence, rubbing his head.

"A formal complaint will not be necessary, Achmed," the policeman says. "We will see that these two are deported immediately."

Turn to page 73.

You run to the old wooden door. A weathered sign is covered with faded words in Arabic. You both push open the door and stumble inside as another boulder smashes to the street behind you.

You find yourself in some sort of warehouse. The large room is dimly lit by a single light bulb suspended from a rafter. You walk forward slowly to inspect the barrels that fill the room.

"They're filled with grain," you tell Indy. "Wheat and barley, I think. Are we safe in here?"

A strange voice from behind you in the dark warehouse answers the question. "The answer is *no*!" he calls out.

Turn to page 24.

You hear the crack of ancient bones as the mummies stagger forward. The air smells musty and stale. An arm falls off one of the mummies and hits the floor with a thud. Another mummy loses its head, but it doesn't stop coming toward you.

"Let's go!" you cry, horrified.

You and Indy turn and begin to run to the door.

But the door has been closed and locked by one of the black-robed men. He leers at you in triumph. You search for another exit as the mummies stagger forward. The air is foul. The floor is littered with their rotted arms and legs.

And still they come.

You have no choice but to fight them.

Turn to page 78.

Ouch! OUCH!!

The whip wasn't strong enough to carry you both at once. Why didn't you go one at a time?

You both fall back to the floor, and— OUCH!

Those scorpions don't seem glad you dropped in!

OUCH!

This adventure has come to a painful conclusion.

The Pyramid of Rhamahr will hold its ancient secrets, it appears, until the next time you open the book.

THE END

"Quick! Tilt the mummy cases back! Maybe they'll float!" Indy yells. The two of you begin to push back the mummy cases, turning them into boats. The silent, ancient passengers bob up and down, safe from the rising water

"I don't see any mummy case for *us* to take!" you yell.

"How good a swimmer are you?" Indy asks, the water up to his chest now.

"Not bad," you reply.

"Let's try to swim out of here!" Indy yells. The deep water is swirling around the room. You cannot see Salaam or any of the cult members. They must have drowned in the raging floodwaters.

Trying not to think about them, you swim as hard as you can in the churning water. The waves keep pushing you back, but you don't give up.

Suddenly you see a mummy case floating several yards to your right. Is it empty? Will it carry you to safety? You are almost to the doorway. Maybe you should just continue swimming.

Quick—make your decision.

Keep swimming? Turn to page 91.
Try to reach the mummy case? Turn to page 117.

46

Desperately Indy shoves away pieces of the wooden desk and searches the carpet for a trap door. You dash to the wall and begin to run your hands across it.

The gas is thick and sour smelling. You cough and choke as you reach the nearest bookshelf. Your lungs feel ready to burst. You can't take another breath. The room begins to spin.

You grab on to the bookshelf to hold yourself up...

...and a small door slides open in the wall!

"Quick, Indy! I've found it!" you manage to sputter.

You stagger forward into the opening and find yourself in a dark tunnel. Indy is right behind you.

"Marla—this way!" he calls.

"But it's dark in there—and filthy!" she cries, choking and gasping for breath.

Indy reaches through the small opening and pulls her in. The three of you stumble forward in the darkness.

What is that fluttering noise coming toward you?

Turn to page 17.

Indy ducks and plunges a fist into the huge man's stomach. The man doesn't seem to notice that he's been hit.

Indy tries hitting him again. The giant stares back defiantly at Indy. He tilts his head back in triumphant laughter. Indy takes this opportunity to give him a shove.

The man stumbles backward, loses his balance, and falls. The boulder drops away from him and crashes through the roof.

"We've got him now!" Indy yells. He tosses you his pistol. "Keep this on him!" He leaps onto the giant and tries to pin him to the roof.

The huge man yells in protest, but Indy has the advantage now. "Maybe you'd like to explain what's going on!" Indy demands.

"He won't explain anything, Jones!" A man's voice rasps behind you. "Drop the gun, kid."

You drop the gun. You turn your head and see three men, all in black robes, their faces covered with black scarves. They are holding pistols aimed right at you.

You and Indy look at each other. You know by his expression that you both have the same idea—to escape by the only route available. You're going to leap off the roof and try to make it to the next rooftop!

Turn to page 61.

A mummy makes a grab for you, and Indy shoves it out of the way. You fall to the floor as another mummy swings an ancient fist.

You're on all fours now, crawling as quickly as you can toward the secret door. You turn and see that Indy is right behind you.

A black-robed man stands in your way. You leap to your feet and butt him in the stomach with your head. He falls backward with a loud *oof*.

You've reached the small doorway. You run through it. You find yourself in a dark tunnel.

You turn to see if Indy is right behind you. You hear Marla Evans scream, but you don't see Indy.

The door slams shut behind you.

You are trapped in the dark tunnel by yourself!

What is that snarling sound behind you??

Turn to page 83.

"This can't be happening!" you cry. "It's—it's a nightmare! Pinch me!"

"Oooh—the smell!" Marla cries as the odor of decay fills the chamber.

The three of you stare in disbelief as the ancient mummies stagger and stumble toward you, their gauzed arms breaking free of their crumbling bonds, stretching out menacingly toward you.

The cats begin to howl and cry. You are backed up almost to the doorway.

Indy slides his bullwhip down from his shoulder. "We may have to give these old guys a fight," he says.

You must decide what to do.

....

Try to fight them? Turn to page 23.

Try to run out of the secret passage and get away from them? Turn to page 60.

You fall back onto the mummy case, clutching the papyrus tightly in both hands. A black-robed man throws himself on top of you. Indy is right behind him.

The black-robed man makes a grab for the papyrus.

You pull back.

The ancient papyrus crumbles in your hands. The small, dry pieces fall to the floor.

The black-robed men are screaming in sorrow and dismay.

The mummies have fallen, still and lifeless. They will move no more.

Indy grabs his bullwhip. He easily rounds up the dispirited cult members.

"More than a thousand years ago members of the Cult of Rhamahr claimed to have the secret of bringing mummies back to life," Indy says. "Up until this very moment no one realized they were telling the truth!"

"And no one else will ever believe it," you say regretfully, running your fingers through the tiny pieces of the papyrus that held the amazing secret.

"I'm still not sure that *I* believe it," Marla Evans says. "This all seems like some sort of bizarre adventure tale."

Searching the cases across the room, Indy finds the two mummies missing from the National Museum. "It's a bizarre adventure tale, all right," Indy says, grinning, "and I'm happy to say it's one that's come to

THE END.

You grab torches off the wall of the entrance chamber and run into the dark unknown, through the doorway on the right and into...

...another dark chamber. You search the walls and floor of this chamber. It is empty. There is one doorway on the far wall.

"I guess we have no choice this time," Indy says. "That's strange. Pyramids don't have wooden doors. This door was obviously put here recently."

The door is latched but not locked. Indy pulls the latch and pushes in the door. You step inside.

It is dark at first. You hold up your torches.

You find yourself staring at two snarling tigers. The snarls become roars. "I—I don't think they want company!" you cry.

"These are Bengal tigers," says Indy as calmly as if he were lecturing. "I can't imagine what Bengal tigers are doing here...unless they are part of the Rhamahr ceremony."

The tigers pace back and forth, staring at you, snarling their displeasure. Your back is pressed against the chamber wall. "Let's get out of here!" you cry, edging your way to the wooden door.

But the door has closed behind you. You can't budge it!

....

Turn to page 65.

The secret door in the wall is controlled by a timed spring lock. After you entered the secret passageway, the door closed and locked behind you.

You have no choice but to go forward into the dark passage.

You didn't really think you'd be allowed to escape danger so easily, *did you*?"

Stop stalling and turn to page 27.

The truck stops suddenly. You jump down and look for cover. "Wow!" you cry. You are standing in the shadow of a tall brick pyramid.

"Yeah, just like in the history books," Indy says.

The truck doors are opening. You cannot find a place to hide.

Should you duck under the truck and hope you won't be seen? Or make a dash for the pyramid and hope there's a place to hide inside?

Climb under the truck? Turn to page 84.
Run to the pyramid? Turn to page 94.

The black-robed man bursts into the chamber, waving the small, black pistol in his hand at you and Indy. "Dirty invaders of the sacred Hall of Rhamahr, prepare to die!" he yells.

You and Indy step to the side and lower your torches.

The tigers immediately attack the man. As they leap onto him, you turn away. You do not wish to see them take their meal.

"Let's go—now!" Indy yells. The tigers do not look up as you and Indy run out the door.

You run blindly through a long, low tunnel. You run until you see a dim light. Then you run toward the light...

...which turns out to be the torches of four other black-robed men!

They grab you both and tie your hands behind you.

"Take them to the New Pharaoh!" one of them cries, shoving you forward toward the entrance to a vast, brightly lit chamber.

Turn to page 3.

THUDDDDDD! THUDDDDDD!

Five stories below, you land in an oxcart filled with wheat.

In front of the cart, the farmer yells at his ox to speed up. He cannot understand why the poor ox has suddenly stopped.

"Get down! Get down!" Indy whispers. The two of you bury yourselves deep in the wheat as bullets begin to whiz above your heads.

A few moments later the shooting has stopped. The farmer urges his ox on, not realizing that the load has grown somewhat heavier. He drives the cart right through the center of Cairo.

When you are in front of the Cairo Museum, Indy climbs out of the wheat. "We'll get out here, driver!" he calls.

The farmer is too startled to talk as the two of you climb out of his cart.

"Well, we've reached our destination," Indy says as the two of you begin to climb the steps to the museum. "That was easy, wasn't it?"

Why are you in Cairo?

Turn to page 87.

A mummy grabs Indy around the waist and begins to squeeze. Indy's face turns red and his eyes bulge as he struggles to free himself from the ancient being's powerful grip.

A mummy steps in front of you. Its head rolls backward and falls to the floor. Your headless adversary makes a grab for you.

You duck under the moldy arms. You see the papyrus lying on the floor where the black-robed man dropped it. You don't see how it will help you, but you decide to do as Marla said.

You duck away from another swipe of the mummy's arms and leap toward the papyrus.

It's almost in your grasp...

...when a black-robed man kicks it out of your reach.

Turn to page 12.

What happened to Salaam?

Why were the mummies stolen from the National Museum?

These are questions that you will not be able to answer in this adventure, for you have made a bad choice.

Did you forget that gas rises?

Climbing up to the window was not a wise move. You were safer staying down low.

You'll be choked up to learn that this breathtaking episode has come to an end.

Make a last-gasp effort to close the book. Then try a different path. With luck, next time you'll be able to breathe new life into the legend of Indiana Jones!

THE END

The cats are screeching and howling. The mummies have you surrounded. One of them reaches out a long arm and bats the whip from Indy's hand.

The mummies move in for the attack. Marla gasps and falls back against the wall. You raise your hands in front of your face. You don't want to see what happens next. You wait...

...and wait.

Nothing happens next.

The mummies have all stopped. They slowly slump to the floor.

"They've lost their energy," Indy says, wiping sweat from his brow with his hat. "And listen—the cats have stopped howling. They seem to be connected to the mummies somehow. We've got to get going. We don't have time to figure this out. They may start moving again!"

The three of you stumble out the doorway. You are exhausted, but you make your way as quickly as you can through another dark passage. A few seconds later, you find yourself in another secret chamber of the Cairo Museum.

"Indy, look—" you cry. "More mummies!"

Will these mummies attack too?

Turn to page 14.

You lower your head and run as fast as you can. You and Indy reach the edge of the roof at the same time. You grab on to the low concrete wall and prepare to jump.

But there is one little problem.

The next rooftop is three stories below.

Indy quickly turns away from the edge of the roof and grabs the huge man, who is still struggling to his feet. "Get behind him, kid," Indy says, using the giant as a shield. "We're walking away from here—with him in front of us! They're not going to shoot their own man!"

You get behind Indy and the huge, protesting human shield.

The three men in black robes stare angrily at you. They raise their pistols...

Turn to page 80.

"Oh, I'm sorry, Dr. Salaam. I had no idea you had visitors." The intruder is a young blond woman, dressed in a smart gray business suit and carrying a notepad.

"Come in, come in, Marla," Salaam says, giving her the same thin-lipped smile he gave you and Indy. "I believe you will find Mr. Jones's story of interest. This is Marla Evans, my assistant," Salaam says turning to Indy. "She is an American too."

"I'm from Cincinnati," Miss Evans says, looking Indy up and down. His rumpled clothes covered with grains of wheat obviously do not impress her.

"How exciting for you," Indy says sarcastically. He turns to Salaam. "Can we get down to business? We're here on a rather urgent matter."

"Yes, yes," Salaam says, pointing to a chair for Miss Evans. She pulls the chair as far away from Indy and you as possible and sits down primly, her back as straight as the chair back.

"Dr. Salaam, I'm here because two mummies were recently stolen from the National Museum," Indy says.

He is interrupted by a loud crash!

Turn to page 90.

OUCH!!!!

Did you forget about the hot tar that was beginning to pour from the cart?

Too bad.

Staying in the pit put you in a rather sticky situation—and brought this adventure to its burning conclusion!

THE END

The green gas is pouring quickly into the room now. You begin to cough and your eyes are burning.

Indy tries the door again, pulling as hard as he can. It won't budge.

"The window!" he yells, looking up at the small window high above Salaam's shattered desk.

"The window is barred," Marla says. "All of the windows in the museum are barred."

"We've got to try it anyway. Maybe we can break through," Indy says, holding his filthy handkerchief up over his nose and mouth.

"Dr. Salaam! We've got to get him out too!" you say. You look down to see if Salaam is moving.

He has moved, all right.

He has completely disappeared!

"Indy—Salaam—he's gone!" you cry.

....

Turn to page 36.

You both pull on the door with all your strength. "Seems to have a spring on it," Indy says. "I think it's just jammed. But I don't think we have time to try to pry it open. Those tigers look hungry to me!"

The tigers have stopped pacing. They raise back their heads and roar out a final warning. They are about to attack.

Indy pulls his bullwhip off his shoulder. "We can either try to teach them some manners with this," he says, "or try to keep them back with these torches while we work on prying the door open."

You must decide how you will defend yourselves against the hungry tigers.

Use the bullwhip? Turn to page 96.
Use the torches? Turn to page 114.

You try to throw him another spear, but you cannot get it out of the display case. The black-robed man attacks furiously and, holding the spear at either end, pins Indy to the floor. He begins to press the spear down on Indy's neck, suffocating him.

You leap onto the attacker's back and struggle to pull him off Indy. But he is too strong. He swats you away with a powerful swing of his arm. You fall backward. Indy struggles to get out from under the spear, but he cannot.

You pick yourself up and prepare to leap onto the black-robed attacker again—just as two Cairo policemen run into the room.

The attacker loosens his grip on the spear long enough for Indy to scramble away. The policemen pull out pistols and call out something that sounds like "Freeze!" in Arabic.

"They must've heard the explosion!" Indy croaks, his throat carrying the spear mark emblazoned in red.

What do you do now? Keep fighting and hope that the two policemen will come to your aid? Or take this opportunity to try to escape?

Keep fighting? Turn to page 92.
Escape? Turn to page 107.

You and Indy are tied to pillars in the center of the chamber. "You will watch as I bring our ancient ancestors to life!" the New Pharaoh yells down at you. "And when the mummies walk, they will step forward to put you to your deaths!"

"He's gotta be kidding," Indy mutters to you.

"I don't suppose you have a plan for getting us out of this," you ask hopefully.

"Not at the moment," Indy replies.

A large fire has been built. The New Pharaoh has begun chanting. He holds his scepter over the head of each of the mummies in the chamber. Large leaves are burned in the fire. The New Pharaoh chants again. And then he speaks:

"Now all will witness the miracle of rebirth! My powers will triumph over death! The dead shall walk! Our ancestors, the pride of Ancient Egypt, will walk forward and defeat our enemies!" He calls out a final command to the mummies.

The vast chamber is silent. No one moves. All eyes are on the mummies.

Will they walk?

Turn to page 40.

It's a female voice.

The doctor drops the gas mask, and it falls to the floor. You look up and see Marla Evans holding a pistol. She looks terribly out of place in her prim gray suit and gray pumps, standing in this dusty pyramid chamber, holding a pistol. But out of place or not, you're certainly glad to see her.

"Release them!" she orders. She waves the pistol menacingly. Two black-robed men rush forward and untie you and Indy.

"Miss Evans, how—" Indy is actually speechless.

"I figured you might be in some danger. I borrowed the museum staff car and followed the truck's tire tracks."

"I'd say that Dr. Salaam has a very capable assistant in you," Indy says, massaging his burned hand.

"Where is Dr. Salaam, anyway?" Marla asks. "What have they done to him?"

But before you can answer, the man in the mummy costume raises a pistol and fires it at Marla Evans!

Turn to page 81.

The narrow tunnel leads down into a low chamber.

The flame of your torch grows smaller. You keep following the wall to your right. You find yourself in another narrow tunnel. It leads down and then up again.

"I'm sure we'll come to their headquarters soon," you say to Indy. You are trying to reassure yourself.

Indy frowns and keeps walking.

Turn to page 88.

With lightning speed Indy rolls over and grabs the ankles of the servant behind him. He pulls. The man falls over backward. His pistol hits the floor and bounces away.

Indy makes a grab for it—and misses.

Four black-robed men leap onto Indy's back. They punch him with their fists, pounding furiously again and again until Indy is nearly unconscious.

The escape attempt has failed.

You and Indy are dragged down the long carpet until you are a few feet in front of the New Pharaoh, who stands before his throne, staring down angrily at you.

"You cannot escape the wrath of Rhamahr, and you cannot escape the fate chosen for you by the New Pharaoh!" he bellows. "Prepare them for mummification!"

Servants pull you to your feet. A section of the floor begins to move. The floor pulls back, revealing a deep pit. Servants enter from a chamber behind the throne. They are pulling a tall cart. The cart is filled with boiling tar.

"Afraid?" asks the New Pharaoh mockingly. "I will bring you back to life once you have become mummified. You will serve me well!"

"Perhaps we could just forget the whole thing," Indy calls up to him. "You know, let bygones be bygones!"

"Put them in the pit!" the New Pharaoh commands.

Turn to page 105.

Indy stares sullenly out to sea as the small ship makes its way through the dark waters, carrying you back to the United States. Every few minutes he reaches up to massage the huge bump on his head and scowls angrily.

"I take back what I said about this being an educational trip," you say sadly. "I didn't even get to see the pyramids!"

You seem to have made some wrong choices. This adventure is over before it begins.

Well...it's *almost* over. You feel yourself beginning to get extremely seasick.

Things couldn't get worse, could they?

Quick—close the book before you find out!

THE END

You hear the howling again. "Look—inside those little cages!" you cry. Your eyes are adjusting to the dim light. You can make out shelves containing dozens of small cages along the wall of this secret chamber.

The three of you walk up to the cages.

"Cats," Indy says. "Dozens of house cats."

"Why would anyone in the museum keep cats in cages?" Marla asks.

"Good question," Indy replies. "Do you know of any experimenting that's being done with animals?"

Marla doesn't get a chance to answer.

You hear a muffled clumping sound behind

you in the dark room. You turn around to see a group of mummies—living mummies!—lumbering toward you!

Turn to page 51.

You and Indy run over to Salaam. He is badly injured. His head is bleeding. He has already lost a lot of blood. Indy loosens Salaam's tie and props up his head on a broken piece of the shattered desk.

"The papyrus..." Salaam croaks, struggling to form the words. "Go...the mummy room...the papyrus..."

"What papyrus?" Indy asks. "What about a papyrus?"

Salaam's eyes roll back in his head.

"He's dead," Indy says.

"This is horrible, horrible!" Marla cries. She looks up to see Indy running from the office. "Where are you going?"

"To the mummy room," he answers without slowing down. "Salaam seemed to know what this was all about. I hope we can find out—in time!"

Quick—run to the mummy room!

Turn to page 113.

"We don't have time to save the mummies!" Indy cries. "If we don't get outta here fast, we'll be underwater!"

You see a large wooden chest floating near the far wall. You make your way toward it, through water that's already up to your shoulders. You swim, then reach out until you grab on to the wooden chest.

"Nice goin', kid," Indy says, swimming up to you. "That looks like it should hold us both up pretty well."

You look over and see Salaam sinking under the water. It is the last time you will ever see him.

A few moments later you are floating out of the pyramid. You and Indy hold on to the chest. It keeps you afloat as you guide it by kicking your legs.

"Hold on tight, kid," Indy says. "The water is starting to recede. Just yell 'Land ahoy' if you see anything that looks dry."

You look around. You don't see anything that looks dry. The river waters have flooded this entire low-lying area.

Will you make it to land?

Turn to page 109.

The mummies are only a few feet away. Their stench is overpowering. You struggle to breathe. They form a circle around you and Indy. The black-robed men look on with smiling faces.

Indy raises his whip and brings it down across the chest of one of the advancing mummies. It seems to have no effect. The mummy doesn't even slow its advance.

Craaaaack! Craaaaack!

Indy brings the whip down again and again.

A mummy reaches forward with an ancient, gauze-covered hand and swats the whip away. Indy turns to you in astonishment. "These guys are strong!" he cries.

You back away from them. But you don't have much room to back up.

Suddenly a display case against the far wall begins to move. It's a hidden door!

Marla Evans steps into the room.

Will she be able to save you?

Turn to page 19.

"And whom have we here?" the mummy asks. His voice sounds familiar.

"You can't get away with this!" Indy yells. "That's a very clever costume you're wearing. But you're not clever enough to get away with stealing these mummies!"

"Hahahaha!" The mummy gives a long, dry laugh. "How convenient that you have come. Come closer. I won't harm you—for a while. Hahaha!"

The cult members force you to walk up to the man in the mummy costume. "Indy, I know I've heard that voice somewhere," you whisper.

Through the dirty brown gauze that covers his face, the mummy's eyes peer deeply into yours. "Your sacrifice will be great. But the scientific achievement will be greater," he says, staring at you. "The sacred mummies of our ancient motherhood will once more walk the earth in all of their majesty."

"And just what will we be sacrificing?" Indy asks defiantly.

"Your brains," the mummy replies. "Let the operation begin at once." He turns to his men. "Bind them both to the altar. Prepare to transfer their brains into the chosen bodies of our beloved ancestors!"

Turn to page 101.

...and fire! The giant cries out in agony and slumps to the rooftop.

"Guess that wasn't one of my best theories," Indy says, watching as the three assailants close in.

"Any new theories?" you ask.

"We can either fight or jump," Indy says flatly.

Which do *you* choose—fight them or jump down three stories to the next rooftop?

Fight? Turn to page 11.
Jump? Turn to page 93.

The shot misses. But it frightens Marla, and she drops her gun.

Indy kicks the pistol from the fake mummy's hand. He punches the impostor in the jaw. "OWWWWWWW!" Indy forgot about his burned hand!

The black-robed men move toward Marla Evans. But you pick up the pistol from the floor. "Stand right there or I'll shoot!" you scream. Everyone freezes once more.

Indy reaches over with his good hand and rips the gauze off the mummy's face. "Here is Dr. Salaam," he says.

Marla gasps in shock. "The explosion—the blood..."

"All faked for our benefit," Indy says. "But we weren't exactly thrown off the track, Salaam." Salaam scowls and looks away. "Come on, kid. Help me round up these mummy lovers. We'll get them to the Cairo police. Then we'll see about sending the mummies back where they belong. Our job here is finished, I'm happy to say."

"It was fun while it lasted," you say.

"Kid, you've got a weird sense of fun," Indy says. "I like that. I like that a lot!"

As you ride back to Cairo you take a long last look as the pyramid fades into the distance. You know it is a sight you will never forget.

THE END

You toss the ancient papyrus to Indy. He fumbles it, then grabs it tightly.

The mummies all turn to face him. Indy studies the writing on the papyrus. Can he read it?

Yes!

He calls out a command.

The mummies turn and begin to go after the men in black robes. "Hey—this really works!" Indy cries in surprisc.

While he is acting so pleased with himself, a man in a black robe grabs the papyrus from his hand.

Turn to page 103.

Your eyes adjust slowly to the darkness. You pound on the door that just closed behind you. You try to find a door handle, a lever—anything to open it! But you cannot get it to budge.

You hear the snarling sound again.

You turn and stare. Slowly your eyes begin to focus on...

...the snarling face of a SIX-FOOT-TALL RAT!

The rat bares long fangs, opens wide its drooling mouth, and moves forward to attack its prey—you!

Everything goes black.

Turn to page 110.

You hit the sand and squeeze under the truck. The bottom of the truck is as hot as the desert sand. You feel as if you're being toasted on both sides.

But you have no time to think about how uncomfortable you are. You lie as still as possible and pray that you won't be seen.

From your vantage point you see the sandaled feet of the men in black robes as they climb out of the truck. These must be the cult members that Salaam had begun to tell you about. Some of them walk directly into the low, dark entrance to the pyramid. Others struggle to remove something from the truck above you.

The stolen mummies!

You watch in silence as the ancient mummies are gently placed on the sand and then carried toward the pyramid.

Almost all of the cult members have entered the pyramid now. In a few seconds you will be safe, you tell yourself.

And then you sneeze.

Turn to page 112.

"Lock them up in the tomb of Rhamahr!" the New Pharaoh commands. He raises his scepter high in the air. "I will allow you to spend eternity in the resting place of our great leader."

"Very generous of you!" Indy calls out. He turns to you. "Kid, I think we'd better make our break now."

Indy shoots back his elbows and breaks the grasp of the black-robed servant holding him. The servant holding you makes an unsuccessful grab for Indy, leaving you free to escape.

Indy runs at full speed down the carpet toward the New Pharaoh, knocking guards out of his path. You try to follow him, but you are quickly caught by a group of guards.

Indy gets almost to the platform where the New Pharaoh stands, his scepter still in the air. But he is tripped, falls to the ground, and is captured once again.

"Insolent dogs!" the New Pharaoh cries angrily. "Now I will make you wish you had not attempted to defy my will!"

Turn to page 67.

A few minutes later you find yourself entering the plush, bookshelf-lined office of the curator of the Cairo Museum. "Come right in, Mr. Jones," says a tall, dark man with slicked-back, straight black hair, a pencil moustache, and a thin-lipped grin. He comes out from behind his large mahogany desk. "I do not believe we have met. I am Omar Salaam."

Indy shakes hands with Dr. Salaam and introduces you. Salaam offers you chairs in front of his desk. "My old friend Marcus Brody from the National Museum wired me that you were coming, Jones. Have you been visiting our farms, perchance?"

Indy is puzzled at first. Then he realizes what Salaam is talking about. "Oh, you mean this wheat?" Indy says, brushing a few grains off his shoulder onto Salaam's plush red carpet. "No...uh...we took a shortcut here."

"I am quite curious as to why you and your friend are here, Mr. Jones," Salaam says. "Please tell your story."

But before Indy can begin, the door to Salaam's office bursts open.

Turn to page 62.

The tunnel leads to a large, empty chamber. Another rat scurries in front of your feet. You keep walking, into another winding tunnel. The light of your torch grows even dimmer.

"The Pharaohs feared that their tombs would be looted," Indy says quietly as you walk. "Sometimes they built endless mazes into their pyramids. They wanted trespassers to get lost in the endless maze so that the sacred burial chamber with all its treasures would not be violated."

Have you and Indy been unlucky enough to walk into an endless maze?

Turn to page 71.

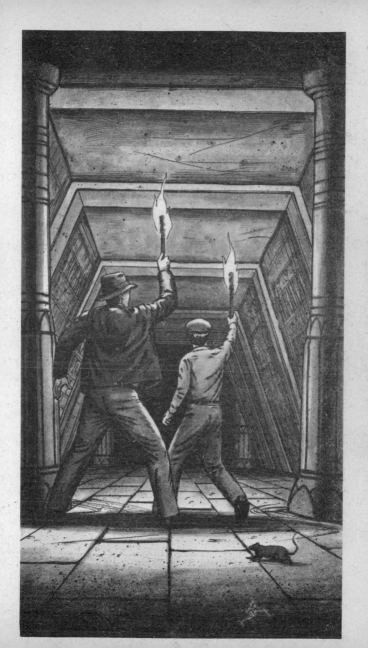

Salaam rushes to the office door and pulls it open. A servant is outside, bending over a tray of drinks that he has just dropped. "Terribly sorry, effendi," he says, shrugging his shoulders.

"Was he eavesdropping?" Indy asks suspiciously after Salaam has closed the door again.

"I do not believe so," Salaam replies quietly. "He is a trusted menial. Continue, Jones."

"We have information that the two stolen mummies were brought to Egypt. We don't know why or by whom. Marcus Brody has asked me to find them and get them back for the National Museum."

"And why has this young person accompanied you?" Salaam asks, looking at you with a frown.

"My young cousin here was visiting me for the summer, so I brought him along."

Marla Evans sneezes. Indy offers her his filthy handkerchief and she recoils in disgust.

"I believe I can be of help to you regarding the stolen mummies," Salaam says, his face turning grim. "I think you need to know about the Cult of Rhamahr!"

Turn to page 104.

You are swimming harder than you've ever swum in your life. Your eyes are closed. You do not think about breathing, about seeing, about anything but pulling yourself forward.

Slowly the force of the water seems to weaken. "Keep goin', kid," Indy yells. "The water's receding. We're gonna make it!"

Indy's right. A few minutes later you are swimming outside the pyramid. Indy floats up beside you. "We've made it so far," he says, "but it's a long way back to town. We'll never make it the rest of the way."

"Mr. Jones! Oh, Mr. Jones!" You hear a female voice calling.

It's Marla Evans! She's standing at the prow of a small barge, a barge manned by Cairo policemen!

"Mr. Jones, what on earth!" she cries.

"We're just enjoying a swim in the local waters," Indy says as you both paddle over to the small boat. "Did you bring the beach towels?"

She backs away as the two of you climb into the barge, your clothes filthy from the overflowing river and floating debris.

"Miss Evans, you have saved our lives," Indy says with a grin. "How can I ever repay you?"

"Just don't come near me!" she replies quickly, holding a handkerchief up to her nose.

THE END

Indy yells something in Arabic to the two policemen and leaps at the black-robed man. The man ducks away and Indy hits the marble floor. He shakes his head, a bit dazed.

Before he can recover, two gunshots ring out. The policemen cry out and drop to their knees. They have been shot from behind. Without looking back, the black-robed man runs past them and through the door from which the shots were fired.

"Come on—after him!" Indy cries, pulling himself to his feet.

"I'm a journalist," Marla protests. "I don't *chase* people!" But she follows you as you run after the black-robed man.

You reach the back exit of the museum. "Stand back," Indy warns, motioning you back with his hand. "There are a lot of them, all in black robes. I can't see Salaam. They must have him, though. They're piling into a truck."

"Let's not stand here! Let's go!" you cry.

"Wait...just a moment..." Indy says, watching them from the doorway. "Give them a chance to get into their truck."

You wait a few more seconds, your heart pounding.

"Okay! Run!" Indy yells.

The three of you begin to run toward the truck just as it pulls away. "Grab on to the back! Let's go for a ride!" Indy yells.

Can you do it?

Turn to page 20.

Without looking back, you leap off the roof. You drop down to the roof below. "Safe!" you tell yourself. But you've spoken to yourself too quickly.

These old Egyptian roofs were not built to have people skydiving onto them!

The roof breaks beneath your weight and you crash through to the apartment below—which belongs to a rather distressed Cairo policeman.

There have always been strict laws for breaking and entering in Egypt. In ancient days you might have had your hands cut off for the crime you just committed.

But since this is your first offense, they go easy on you. You receive a prison term of only five hundred years.

Just think—sometime in the 2430s you'll be able to finish this adventure!

THE END

"Keep down low, kid," Indy whispers, "and run straight to the entrance. Maybe they won't see us."

You want to ask, "What do we do once we're inside?" But there's no time for discussing plans.

You lean low into the shadow of the truck and take a deep breath. Then, in a sudden burst of speed, digging your feet deep into the sand, you run straight toward the entrance. Indy is a few paces ahead. Neither of you looks back to see if you've been spotted.

The low opening on the side of the pyramid is just a few yards ahead of you now. Ten more seconds and you'll enter the safety of its darkness.

"HEY—" yells a voice behind you. And then the loud, angry voice calls out something in Arabic.

You've been spotted!

ge 10.

You run to the office door and struggle to pull it open. Indy is right behind you.

"Let me try it, kid," he says. He turns the knob and pulls with all his might. "It's been secured from the outside," he says, giving up. "We're locked in here!"

"What's that hissing sound?" Marla Evans asks, walking up behind you.

You look down. "Gas!" you yell. Green gas is seeping into the room from under the door.

"We're trapped! Trapped!" Marla cries in terror.

Turn to page 64.

Indy lifts the bullwhip and cracks it loudly. He raises it again and snaps it over the head of one of the tigers.

Unfortunately the tigers are not afraid of the whip and its sounds. In fact it angers them even more. They are too hungry to care about a little insignificant whip cracking.

You, on the other hand, will probably lose your appetite if you keep reading. Perhaps this unfortunate episode has given you food for thought. Open the book again when you are hungry for adventure—and ready to make some better choices!

THE END

"Who screamed?" Indy asks.

"Not me!" you insist.

You reach up, grab the top of the pit, and pull yourself up so you can see what's going on in the chamber.

It's the tigers!

The two Bengal tigers must have followed the voices to the New Pharaoh's chamber—and they still seem to be hungry!

One black-robed servant lies bloodied and maimed on the carpet. The tigers prowl, looking for their next victim. The room is filled with screams of terror as servants run in all directions.

The New Pharaoh stands frozen in fear. The tigers are eyeing him now.

What will *you* do? Stay in the pit till the tigers have had their meal? Or use this opportunity to escape?

Wait the tigers out? Turn to page 63.
Try to escape? Turn to page 6.

The servant chants quietly. You and Indy stand frozen, listening to the strange-sounding words.

He stops. He drops the papyrus to the floor and turns his eyes to the mummy cases.

Slowly, seemingly with great effort, the mummies raise their arms. Then they slowly, agonizingly, take a step forward out of their cases.

The mummies are walking now. They leave footprints of ancient dust as they move forward, their rotted arms outstretched.

"Like mummies in a horror movie!" you think.

But this is no movie. This is actually happening before your startled yes.

The black-robed servant calls out a command.

The mummies turn. They begin to walk toward you. Their heads roll around on their necks. They have no eyes. But they are moving toward you as if by instinct.

Indy's eyes do not move from the hideous approaching figures. He slowly removes the bullwhip from his shoulder.

"Maybe we should just get out of here!" you suggest.

You must decide. Battle the ancient mummies? Or run?

· ·

Fight? Turn to page 78.
Run? Turn to page 44.

99

Grabbing the torches and using them to fend off your captors might have been a good idea—except for the unfortunate fact that the torches were built right into the wall.

You gave the three black-robed men a good laugh with that one!

They also seemed to enjoy tossing you into the bottomless pit, one of the more dangerous attractions in this particular pyramid.

It was a good day for them.

And a bad day for you (unless you get a thrill out of falling forever).

Perhaps the next time you drop into the pyramid you will fall into better luck!

THE END

"You're nuts!" Indy yells, struggling to get free of the mummy's men. "The Cult of Rhamahr tried for centuries—and never succeeded in bring a mummy to life."

"The formula they used was incorrect. I have the correct one. And now I have the fresh brains I need to complete our first experiment!" The man in the mummy costume rubs his gauzed hands together in anticipation.

"We have two choices, kid," Indy whispers. "Make a grab for Gauze Face and try to take him hostage. Or try to tilt that steaming pot and pour some hot sauce on him."

The guards grab you by the shoulders and try to push you down onto the altar.

How will you try to escape?

Try to take the talking mummy as hostage? Turn to page 116.

Try to pour the contents of the pot onto him? Turn to page 8.

You keep pulling at the door, but you can't make it budge another quarter of an inch! Then, just as you suggest that maybe you and Indy should trade places, the torches go out.

This isn't good news for you.

Of course, with no lights, the tigers can't see you too well. It'll probably take an extra thirty seconds or so for them to find you in the dark.

Perhaps you should use that thirty seconds to close the book. This adventure is about to come to a truly tasteless conclusion.

THE END

The black-robed man holds the papyrus high and calls out a command. The mummies turn and return to their attack on you and Indy.

"Grab it! Grab the papyrus!" Marla Evans screams.

Indy grabs the papyrus back, dodges away from one of the black-robed cult members, and calls out a command.

The mummies turn again...

...and burst into flames!

"No! No!" everyone in the room cries, seeing these valuable mummies burning to ashes before your eyes.

"Our ancestors are dying!" one of the cult members cries in horror. "The secret of Rhamahr shall die with them!" He grabs the papyrus away from the shocked Indy and tosses it onto one of the burning mummies. The papyrus flares for an instant and then disappears.

The cult members flee the room. You are too busy staring at the last of the burning mummies to pay any attention to them.

"The two mummies stolen from the National Museum were among these," Indy says sadly. "We have seen a miracle here today. But we've paid a high price. I guess this is the end of the Cult of Rhamahr. Without the papyrus, I don't expect anyone will try to bring mummies back to life."

You agree that it is a terrible tragedy. But what a story you've got to tell the kids back home! Think they'll believe you?

THE END

"The Cult of Rhamahr?" Indy asks in surprise. "I know about that cult. It died out centuries ago."

"It has been revived," Salaam says quietly, leaning forward on his desk. "There are people, Jones, who run around in black robes and believe they can bring mummies back to life. They are people who—"

He never finishes his sentence.

A bomb explodes under his desk.

The explosion knocks you out of your chair. Your head hits the carpet with a thud. Everything goes dark. You struggle to regain your feet. The room is filled with smoke.

Indy and Marla Evans are also struggling to their feet. Through the smoke and the wreckage of Salaam's massive desk, you can see Salaam lying motionless on the floor, bleeding.

You hear footsteps. People are running away outside the office door.

Do you chase after them? Or do you first see if you can help Salaam? You'd better decide quickly.

Chase after the footsteps? Turn to page 95.
See if you can help revive Salaam? Turn to page 76.

"Listen, why don't you just keep the mummies?" Indy suggests, beads of perspiration running down his face. "We'll just go home and forget the whole thing."

Six servants grab you and lead you to the edge of the pit. "Prepare to join our ancestors!" the New Pharaoh cries.

A triumphant cheer fills the ancient chamber.

The servants shove you both into the pit. You hit the bottom hard. You are surprised to find that the pit is only about six feet deep. "Deep enough," Indy says grimly. "We have only one hope now, kid."

"What's that?" you ask, your voice trembling.

"That he really can bring us back to life once we're mummified!"

Above you, you can see the cart containing the boiling tar being pushed closer and closer to the pit. The cart comes to a stop right above your heads. It begins to tilt. You can see the bubbling black tar about to pour out.

"AAAAAAIIIIIIIIIIIIEEEEEEEE!"

....

Turn to page 97.

105

Holding his side in agony, Abdul stumbles away as the snake slithers down a hole in the floor.

Abdul pulls open the street door and runs out into the crowded, narrow street, screaming for help.

Indy, still shaken and covered in wheat, slowly picks himself up off the floor. "Nice work, kid," he says, a small grin breaking across his face. "I guess I'm almost glad I brought you along."

"Thanks a bunch," you tell him. You hand him his battered hat.

"Let's get out of here," Indy says, shoving the hat down on his head. "Let's get over to the Cairo Museum and see if we can find out why my old friend Abdul and his pals don't want us around here!"

Turn to page 87.

The black-robed man runs toward the doorway, ignoring the policemen and their commands. The police give chase.

"This is our chance!" Indy cries. "Quick—this way!"

Marla comes running over. Indy runs up to a display case on the far wall. He pulls a small lever beside the case. The wall quickly slides open, revealing a narrow passage.

"Inside!" Indy yells. "I've had my eye on this lever ever since we came into the room!"

The three of you dash inside. The wall closes behind you. You follow the narrow passage into a small, dimly lit chamber.

"I've worked here for two years," Marla says. "I never knew any of this was here. I don't—"

She stops short.

What was that howling sound?

Turn to page 74.

You float in the now still river water for what seems like hours. The sun beams down on you. Your arms grow tired and sore.

Finally the wooden chest that holds you afloat comes to an abrupt stop. "Land ahoy!" you manage to croak.

Indy looks as tired as you do. You both struggle to stand up. You're almost to your feet when your knees buckle. You fall forward, knocking the lid off the chest. Trying to regain your balance you see something sparkling inside the chest.

You pull it out and hand it to Indy, whose eyes grow wide in disbelief. "The rubies of Ramses the Ninth!" he exclaims in awe, holding the red-jeweled necklace tenderly in his hands. "Kid, these jewels are worth more than all the mummies in Egypt!"

"You mean we're rich?" you ask, so excited your weariness disappears and your knees stop wobbling.

"Not exactly...." Indy says, still examining the ancient rubies. "These jewels were on loan to the Cairo Museum. Salaam must've stolen them. All that Cult of Rhamahr nonsense was to keep everyone off the track. With everyone looking for stolen mummies, no one would notice that the jewels had disappeared—until it would be too late to track them down."

Turn to page 111.

A dim light begins to grow from the blackness. Shapes begin to come into focus.

You look up into the worried faces of Indy and Marla Evans. "He's coming to," you hear Indy say. You realize you must have blacked out.

You move your head to get a better view of where you are. You're aware of a tremendous pain in the back of your head. You seem to be in Dr. Salaam's office.

"The explosion..." you say, your throat parched, the words coming out dry and scratchy. "Dr. Salaam...dead...the mummies walking toward us..."

"Take it easy, kid," Indy says. "Dr. Salaam is right here." You see him standing behind Indy and Marla. "There was a loud noise in the hall," Indy explains. "You fell out of your chair. The noise must've frightened you. You hit your head on the desk. It was a nasty crack. You've been out for nearly ten minutes."

"But the mummies walked!" you protest, struggling to sit up.

"You must've been dreaming, kid," Indy says. "We've all been here waiting for you to come out of it."

"I've been waiting for an excuse to go home," Marla Evans says soothingly. "I'm going to take you back to your parents. You'll be fine. Really. You'll be fine."

Fine! Of *course* you'll be fine! But meanwhile you'll miss out on the adventure of your life (unless you close the book and begin again)!

THE END

110

"So that's what rubies look like," you say, watching them sparkle, red and fiery, in Indy's hands. "I guess I'll have a few stories to tell the kids back home."

"I guess you will," Indy says as you start to walk toward town. "Perhaps you could leave out some of the more exciting parts when you tell the story to your parents."

"That's okay," you reply. "If I tell them, they won't believe me anyway!"

THE END

"Sorry, Indy," you say sadly as the two of you are led into the pyramid at gunpoint by three of the black-robed men.

"That's okay, kid," Indy says. "At least you got us a guided tour of this place."

Flaming torches light the walls of the pyramid chamber, casting gray, flickering shadows on the ancient brick walls.

"It smells so musty," you say, coughing in the dusty air.

"Yeah, that's the thing about buildings that are a few thousand years old. They get musty," Indy says.

"Shut up!" one of your captors yells in English, pushing the nose of his pistol into Indy's back.

Now the only sound is that of your shoes scraping against the dusty floor as you walk through the low-ceilinged passages.

You watch Indy's eyes as you walk deeper and deeper into the ancient pyramid. He's looking at the flaming torches that line the walls. Is he about to grab one and use it in an escape attempt? Wouldn't it be smarter to wait until you see where they're taking you? Especially since the three men have guns and are walking less than a foot behind you?"

You must decide.

....

Grab a torch and try to fight them? Turn to page 100.

Play it safe and wait a while? Turn to page 13.

112

You and Indy race through the vast, empty halls of the Cairo Museum. You lose your way once in the maze of corridors. Finally you find the mummy room.

You burst into the room to discover four black-robed men standing before the row of mummy cases. You recognize the servant who dropped the tray outside Salaam's office door. He is standing beside a shattered display case. In his hand he holds a papyrus, which he has obviously just taken from the case.

Ignoring you, he holds up the papyrus and begins to chant the words he sees on it.

"Oh, no!" Indy cries. "I think we're too late!"

Why does Indy look so terrified?

Turn to page 99.

113

You hold the flaming torches in front of you and try to stare the tigers down. "I don't know if the whip would scare them or not," Indy says, staring straight ahead. "But I do know that all animals are afraid of fire."

Indy takes a step forward, then another.

The tigers retreat.

"I'll hold 'em off," he tells you. "See if you can find what's got that door stuck." He thrusts the torch forward. The tigers retreat even more, snarling their displeasure and fear.

You are happy to turn away from the tigers. You bring the torch over to the doorway. You run your hand along the bottom, then along the sides. You cannot find anything.

Again you try pulling with all your strength. The door doesn't budge. You give one more desperate heave. The door moves a fraction of an inch.

"I—I got it to move a little," you call to Indy. "But I have an idea. Why don't I take the torch and set the door on fire? That'll get us out."

Indy is too busy keeping the tigers at bay to hear you. You must decide what to do.

....

Keep pulling at the door now that you've gotten it to move a little? Turn to page 102.

Burn the door down and make a fast exit? Turn to page 25.

Just as Indy reaches for the falling mummy, a guard tries to push him down onto the stone altar. With lightning speed, he slams his elbow into the guard's throat. The guard staggers backward.

Indy picks up one of the large pots of lilies and tosses it at another guard. It catches him on the chest, and he falls to the floor.

Another black-robed guard draws a pistol. You dive into him. He cries out in surprise. The pistol sails across the altar.

"Good goin', kid!" Indy cries.

"Indy, look out!" you yell. Indy doesn't see that the man in the mummy costume has an ancient ceremonial sword in his hand.

The fake mummy reaches back his gauzed arm and plunges the sword deep into Indy's chest!

Turn to page 4.

You turn and swim toward the mummy case, which bobs and spins in the churning waters. You don't know whether Indy is behind you or not.

With great effort you reach the mummy case. You struggle to pull yourself up onto its side. "Not so fast!" a voice yells. A figure sits up in the case. It is Salaam!

He stands up and begins to kick your hands, trying to loosen their grasp on the side of the case. You are exhausted from your efforts. You know you are too tired to swim. You hold on to the side as Salaam kicks at your hands. Using your last ounce of strength, you reach up and grab his leg...

...and pull him into the water!

He begins sputtering and choking. "Help! I can't swim!"

You pull yourself up into the case. "Indy—you're here!" you cry, seeing your cousin swim up to you.

Indy grabs Salaam by the neck in a lifesaver's grip, and he holds on to the side of the case with his other hand. "I think we've just about done it, kid," he says as the mummy case carries the three of you out of the pyramid. "Our job is just about done. What would you like to do to relax when we dump this clown off with the police and get back to Cairo?"

"Uh...anything but go for a swim!" you reply.

And you don't get any argument from Indy on *that* request!

THE END

117